T0077997

Splash of Love

Doris Anne Beaulieu

authorHOUSE

AuthorHouse™
1663 Liberty Drive
Bloomington, IN 47403
www.authorhouse.com
Phone: 833-262-8899

Published by AuthorHouse 04/22/2022

ISBN: 978-1-6655-5808-2 (sc)
ISBN: 978-1-6655-5809-9 (e)

Registered Screenplay

Logline:

A muddy splash disaster leads to a double love story that has to be untwisted both in their own ways. Assumptions hold back opportunities and the pursuit of happiness finally conquers. Two ladies who were college roommates and now business partners realize they have found true love when both men act to save them from a second splash mishap.

Short Synopsis:

This double love story of two ladies who were college roommates who start a business together. This story has confusion and is filled with what if's, laughter and a dash of drama as it unravels the truth for true love to enter.

One business man creates a well thought out plan that gets put into motion not only for himself and his business, but to benefit the whole community. It reaches the point of not only helping through out his state, but working on two neighboring states. It fits the needs of today.

The hobbies of the two business men each in their own fields allow the story to be relatable to all genders. The two men also share their hobbies that surprisingly fall in the interest of their ladies. This romance story is filled with love that will warm your heart in many ways as two lessons of love are learnt. The intensity of what if's becomes real at the end when the two couples meet and the men take action to protect their ladies from a second splash mishap and the girls decide their keepers.

Written and created by:
Doris Anne Beaulieu
doris2@prexar.com

Fade In:

Ext: Early afternoon, Linda is about to cross the road to meet a new business client at Fonder's Club as a limo drives by splashing muddy street water on Ms. Linda Hil

Shaking the muddy water off her blouse and looking up at the limo.

LINDA

Oh no, how rude.

Hearing a voice say "oh no, how rude" Mr. Peter Dash a passenger in the limo looks out the window from the back of the limo.

MR. PETER DASH

"Charles, stop the car."

Mr. Peter Dash steps out of the limo and approaches Linda.

Linda notices the limo stopping, but contines to wipe her clothes as Mr. Peter Dash approaches Linda says:

LINDA

Look what you've done. I have a meeting with a new client and someone in the catering business can't be seen like this. Who drives so close to the edge of the road like that anyway.

Linda is still wiping and checking her body to see if maybe she could button her top suit so it won't look so bad. Peter grabs her wrist to get her attention so she can look at him.

MR. PETER DASH

Miss I live 5 minutes from here. You can clean up, change, and then my driver can take you to your meeting.

Linda looks like she's about to break into tears while still wiping the muddy water off her clothes and occasionally looking up at Peter.

LINDA

I don't walk around with a change of clothes. It's hopeless, I can't go looking like this with a new client. I'll just have to hope they allow me to reschedule and not give this opportunity to someone else.

Peter bends to look Linda in the face as Linda is still looking to wipe anymore water spots she can off herself.

MR. PETER DASH

I have a walk-in closet with clothes about your size.

Linda looks puzzled. Looks up at Peter like she never heard a word he had been saying all along.

LINDA

What?

Mr. PETER DASH

C'mon Miss your wasting time you only have twenty minutes to make that meeting. I have a whole walk in closet of clothes for you to choose from and you'll be able to make your meeting and nothing will be lost.

Linda is very hesitent, but decides to get into the limo with him.

LINDA

Only because this client is important to my business. It's the break we've been looking for and my parner depends on me to bring it in for us.

MR. PETER DASH

So what business are you in?

LINDA

The catering business.

Peter put a big smile on his face like he already knows what meeting she was going to.

MR. PETER DASH

Oh! I see your need now. Here we are I told you just five minutes away.

MR. PETER DASH

Follow me Miss

INT: Linda walking inside the mansion looking around and checking the place out. A maid walks into the room and takes Mr. Peter Dash's coat and hat. Peter looks at Linda and with a hand gesture motions Linda to follow the maid.

MR. PETER DASH

My maid will take you to get cleaned up and changed. You can choose anything you want to wear in the closet and as an apology you may keep it. Charlie my driver will be waiting out front to take you to the meeting once you're ready. Ms. Doris can you make sure Ms....(pause) I'm sorry I never got your name.

3

LINDA

Miss Linda Hill

MR. PETER DASH

Doris will you take Ms. Hill to Susan's room and show her the closet for a change of clothes.

DORIS

Please follow me Ms. Hill

They reach a bedroom that has a huge walk in closet. Linda's Eye's open wide.

(Continuing)

Linda is looking around and spots a dress that she likes. Linda then notices that there is still a price tag on the dress. You watch Linda looking at the clothes and notice they all still have price tags. She decides to find something with a lower price. She finds a pantsuit that will be perfect for the meeting and hurries to get cleaned up. Stops at the full lenght mirror to check herself out before walking out of the room to rush to the limo and get to her meeting.

FADE OUT:

FADE IN:

INT: Linda rushing and getting into the limo.

LINDA

Charles can you please tell your boss I said thank you very much.

CHARLES

Yes Ms. and may I say that outfit looks like a perfect fit for you. I'm sorry about the splash Ms.

EXT: They arrive at Foner's Club. Linda rushing to the door and talking to herself out loud.

LINDA

I didn't even ask his name. What a wife he must have with a closet like that.

INT: Fonder's Club Conference room, at Mr. Peter Dash's head office. Ms. Linda Hill walks in.

MRS. JENNIFER HOSS

(stands up and goes to shake Linda's hands).

JENNIFER

I like your style. My boss and I went shopping and she bought an outfit just like that. Glad to see how well it will fit her.

LINDA

It was a gift.

JENNIFER

I'm Mrs. Jennifer Hoss from Peter Dash enterprise.

(Pause) with a hand gesture.

(continue)

Please, have a seat.

LINDA

I'm Linda Hill from Linda Kara Caterings. You said on the phone this could lead to a permanent assignment. So lets talk first about group size. What type of food are you looking to have, buffet style or table seating?

JENNIFER

We're a large enterprise and pretty much cover all styles of catering. From buffet with finger foods to table served hot dishes. We sometimes have buffets that start with serving sit down orderves. Also cocktail hour with orderves being served in a walk around style before a sit down banquet. Is that something you can handle?

Linda is taking notes as Jennifer talks:

LINDA

Yes we can. On your buffets are we talking finger rolls and cold salads, hot foods or a mixture of both.

JENNIFER

All of the above. I'll let you know as we move along as to the clients we are serving at the time if we take you on as our caterer. Your food needs to meet our approval first. My boss is very big on flavors and knows good food. So no dry food. We have a kitchen to work with so their should never be any reheating of food going on. So if the food and prices are right then you'll be good to go.

LINDA

If you like I can put together a menu to choose from with prices according to rounded off group size or would you prefer it to be according to per person?

JENNIFER

We prefer group size as some do not show up and others have a plus one with them. I usually give you a higher number as any left over we donate to the meals on wheels program.

LINDA

That's very kind of you. Is that something you would want us to package up for you?

JENNIFER

That would be very helpfull for us if you could. Here is their number to call when you have it ready and they are very good at picking it up before kitchen clean up is done. Their only a few miles down the road and apprecite all we do to help them.

LINDA

What style food do you like and don't you ever want to see?

JENNIFER

We serve to a special business clientel so we wouldn't like anything with extra sauces that may drip and stain their clothes and cause any embarassing moments. So please always keep that in mind. Other then that give us a variety. Make our sit down meals two for them to choose from to cover allergies.

You see Linda taking notes on all that is being said to get things right.

LINDA

Do you have any more questions for me or likes and dislikes?

JENNIFER

No, that pretty much takes care of things for me. I look forward to checking out what list you can give me on your foods menu and of course the prices.

LINDA

I'll make a list for sit down meals and buffet style and work the numbers. Give me a few days and I'll also add the price for walking around serving orderves for your happy hour.

JENNIFER

Well, lets start with that and if things look good and your prices are right we will use you on our next sit down dinner that is a group of 50 as a trial. We will see if your food meets our standards here at Peter Dash Enterprise.

LINDA

Thank you for the opportunity to serve you.

Linda shakes Jennifer's hand and leaves.

FADE OUT:

FADE IN:

INT: Evening. Office at catering hall. Linda's partner Ms. Kara Benson walks into the office with an exciting face of wonder and asks.

KARA

Did we get the client? Looks like you went shopping without me girl look at that.

LINDA

Not yet. We have to do a trial banquet first. A group of 50. Why would you think that we got it already?

KARA

Well, look at what you're wearing. That must have cost you at least a few hundred dollars and I must say it looks gorgeous on you.

Kara is pointing to the clothes Linda is wearing.

LINDA

No, some guy's limo driver splashed a puddle of muddy street water on me when I was about to cross the street and he let me get cleaned up at his place.

KARA

You went to a strangers house. Oh my he must have been very handsome with no ring on his hand for you to do that.

LINDA

Kara stop that, he new I was upset trying to get to my meeting and being in the catering business I couldn't show up with mud on me when I'm trying to land a new client. That's all!

KARA

So was he handsome or what?

LINDA

All I remember is his smile and blue eye's. I acted so upset and I'm embarassed about it now. It was childish of me to act like that.

KARA

Did he take you shopping? Come on give me the dirt. What's his name?

LINDA

I only had twenty minutes to get to the meeting that I never even asked his name, and no he didn't take me shopping. I had no time for that.

KARA

So how did you get that expensive outfit?

Kara is opening the jacket to look at the lining and brand.

LINDA

He took me to his mansion that was just five minutes from away and I mean mansion that had a whole walk in closet with price tags still on the clothes and I could pick anyone I wanted.

KARA

That must have been fun to be able to do when we're use to always looking at price tags before we can buy anything. I wish I had gone to just see what the closet looked like to dream a little.

LINDA

Oh I still looked at the price tags for sure and you won't believe the prices. I did take this one that was closer to the bottom on prices so not to look greedy in any way. I like how it fits and easy to move in.

KARA

It does look sharp on you. Too bad you have to return it.

LINDA

Return it to who. I don't even know his name and only remember how the inside of the mansion looked. Beside he told me I could keep what I chose as an appology for the splash. I was in such a hurry I even left my clothes there.

Kara and Linda start laughing.

KARA

Yeah, that sounds like a fair trade.

The girls are still laughing.

(Continue)

So was he handsome or what?

LINDA

Doesn't matter, he's married.

KARA

Did he say it was his wife's closet?

LINDA

No, but why else would he have a closet with a bunch of women's clothes and the bedroom was surely a ladies complete room.

Kara has a very puzzled look on her face.

KARA

Why would he just give his wife's clothes out. Are you sure he's married? Didn't you say all the clothes had price tags on them. Sounds like a puzzle to me.

Linda gives a hand gesture.

LINDA

Stop it. It was his way of apologizing for spalshing me. That's it!

Kara grabs the laptop from the top of the desk.

KARA

Too bad you didn't get a name so we could look him up.

LINDA

I don't know. I'll probably never see him again anyway. We're just a start up and not in that class yet.

KARA

Well we can always dream. Looks like you got a sample of that today.

LINDA

What a mixed up day it was. Now tomorrow we need to get back to work early in the morning and figure out this menu to reach that class of people.

KARA

Let's go over your notes now and think about it tonight so we can start fresh in the morning.

LINDA

They handle a lot of different style meetings and banquets. I think we will need more variety of styles of meals to meet their needs. They seem to be a very big business. It is an enterprise. We may not need other clients if we land this one.

KARA

That would be nice and give us a big boost and you never know the people they serve may want us for some of their parties. This could branch us out in many ways. What have we for do's and don't?

Linda is day dreaming and doesn't hear Kara at all.

(continue)

Earth to Linda. Where are you right now? Did you hear anything I said.

LINDA

I'm confused on something the CEO of the Dash enterprise said at the beginning of the interview.

KARA

What did she say?

LINDA

She made a comment on my outfit I was wearing. That she had gone shopping with her boss and that she bought one just like this and was happy to see how it would fit her boss since she was my size.

KARA

Oh that's not good. I hope we're not done before we even start.

LINDA

So her boss must be his wife. You think she would get upset knowing he gave me an outfit she bought for herself.

KARA

What wife wouldn't?

LINDA

I think I best keep this outfit in the back of the closet and only wear it once I know more about these people.

KARA

That would be best. We need to walk the fine line if we're to land this contract and keep everything strictly business. Now I had as for the do's and don'ts they may have had.

LINDA

Pretty much open to us. They don't want saucy food so it doesn't drip on anyones clothes that might cause embarrassment and sit down meals need to have two entres for people to choose from for allergy reasons.

KARA

Okay, that pretty much covers it for tonight. Let's sleep on it and start fresh in the morning. Good night dream girl.

LINDA

HA HA

You see them turn off the light and shut the door walking out.

FADE IN:

INT: Next day morning Linda is already in the office working when Kara arrives and see's Linda with coffee in hand and the pot is half gone. Kara walks up to the desk before Linda even notices she is there.

KARA

Linda what is going on? Have you been in here all night doing the menu?

LINDA

I came in around four to get this done so we could get this sent out today. Now I need you to do what your good at and work the numbers for me.

KARA

Did you dream about this guy?

LINDA

Yes, But it helped me in the long run as I got to come in and get this done early so you can work and we can save time in getting this to them. The sooner we get it done the faster we know if things are okay.

KARA

I don't understand that fully, but let's run with it. Give me the paperwork and I'll do my stuff and lay off the coffee.

LINDA

I'll go do inventory while you get that done then will have to go get supplies.

INT: Next day at the Catering Office. Linda is at her desk and the phone rings.

LINDA

Hello, Linda Kara's Catering.

JENNIFER

Hello it's Jennifer Hoss from Peter Dash Enterprise. We went over your menu and we decided to go with the Cordon Bleu for the dinner at noon on Friday. I know it's short notice, Can you do it?

LINDA

Yes, we can. Where is the event?

JENNIFER

We have our own banquet room on the backside of this building and you'll see the big parking lot. Banquet room (A) will be the room you will use.

LINDA

How many guest are we serving?

JENNIFER

We're expecting a group of fifty and have a full kitchen that will be available at 8 am.

LINDA

Great, thank you so much for this opportunity. See you then.

FADE OUT:

FADE IN:

INT: Kitchen at Peter Dash Enterprise banquet hall. Noon. Linda is checking all the plates to make sure they look appitising to look at and doing the finishing touches before they get served.

Waiter #1 is coming in the kitcken for more plates that need to be served.

WAITER #1

That speaker is great. Very detailed in what he says.

Waiter #2 walks in the kitcken to get more plates to serve.

WAITER #2

Boy that guy really sounds like he knows a thing or two.

Linda is still busy checking each plate to make sure they look fine as they are trying to land this client permanetly. Waitress #3 walks in and looks at Linda.

WAITER #3

Linda you should be out there listening to him to get some insight. With us being a startup business he does have some good ideas that could help us grow.

Linda takes a peek from the door to see who the guest speaker is. Then pushes herself back into the kitchen real fast talking out loud.

LINDA

It's him again.

Kitchen Cleaning up is going on. As Mr. Peter Dash walks in and Linda is working on packing the leftovers for the Meals on Wheels program and she continues to keep this business like and herself together.

MR. PETER DASH

Well, hello again!

Linda looks up and looking very stunned.

(continuing)

MR. PETER DASH

Your Cordon Bleu seems to be all the people could talk about. I don't think they heard a word I said. I tried it myself and have to agree with them. It was very juicy and tender.

LINDA

I'm sure they heard everything you said. My waiters surely did, but I am gald everyone enjoyed it. I want to thank you for saving me last week before my interview.

MR. PETER DASH

Well I can see it was well worth it the meal was delicious and the service was the quality we like. So thank you!

LINDA

Always happy to please.

MR. PETER DASH

Can I have my limo driver pick you up after your finished up here so we can get some coffee together and talk?

LINDA

I'm sorry I have a lot of work still to do, but it was nice seeing you again.

MR. PETER DASH

Perhaps another time then.

Mr. Peter Dash turns and walks out.

FADE OUT:

FADE IN:

INT: Evening. Back at the cathering office Linda is writting up the bill for the banquet Kara walks in.

KARA

That guess speaker is a hunk. Tall, blue eye's and he came to talk to you. What did he have to say?

LINDA

He told me everyone enjoyed the meal and he liked it himself. Then wanted to take me out for coffee to get to know me better.

KARA

Well I'd jump at that in a minute.

LINDA

Something he said has me puzzled.

KARA

Are you day dreaming girl?

LINDA

No! He said "The quality is what we like" he used the word we.

KARA

He's the guest speaker and we made him look good.

LINDA

Yeah you're probably right, but maybe he's part of the Enterprise as this is the enterprises building and it's his wife's clothes I was wearing on that interview?

KARA

That would be so funny!

LINDA

No it's not. I feel like I'm digging myself into a hole and messing up our chances at getting this client we need. I have to keep this business like and it's getting hard.

KARA

Well it's sure entertaining to me.

LINDA

Thanks a lot partner.

KARA

Hey Linda, tomorrow being saturday, do you have any plans?

LINDA

My laundry and getting organized for next week. Why?

KARA

The Community College is having a small business seminar for catering businesses and it's open to everyone at 2pm. It might give us ideas on cutting costs and growing our business further.

You see the two girls walking out after cleaning the kitchen together still talking.

LINDA

Alright, it wouldn't hurt to check it out and the time works for me.

FADE OUT:

FADE IN:

INT: College auditorium. Afternoon. Linda is late as Kara is still standing at the back wall waiting for her so they can take a seat together. Linda finally walks in.

LINDA

Oh my it's him again.

KARA

You're late and the brochure says his name is Mr. Peter Dash.

LINDA

Are you kidding me! No wonder he has a manson. He's the Peter Dash Enterprise we catered to yesterday. I was right I was wearing his wife's clothes.

KARA

Linda this is so funny, but it's not your fault. His limo driver put all that into motion not you. It's not like you're chasing a married man. Now we have a name and know more about the guy.

(continue)

He has a lot of ideas that could really help save us time and make our record keeping a simple job. I've been taking notes.

LINDA

Great! I know your right, but why do I feel like I'm between a rock and a hard place.

KARA

I think you have a thing for him.

Linda gives Kara a nudge and says.

LINDA

No I don't.

Mr. Peter Dash is at the podium still speaking.

MR. PETER DASH

We have brochures in the back of the room from local farmers about their fresh produce options. You'll find buying in bulk for food you use most will save you time and money. Make sure you compare prices with the venders for the best deals. Your clients will enjoy and be able to taste the difference with fresh food. To save time call ahead and they will pick it right when you need it. Thank you all for coming and help yourself to the refreshments.

Kara finds Linda in a stare and says.

KARA

Are you daydreaming again?

LINDA

Why are all the good ones taken?

KARA

Because they're good.

Laughing!

(continuing)

KARA

Get your head in the game girl.

LINDA

You took notes right?

KARA

Don't look now, but he's coming our way.

Linda looks down pretending to look at pamphlets.

MR. PETER DASH

I see you came in late.

LINDA

Sorry about that the traffic was working against me today. My partner here Kara took notes for us.

MR. PETER DASH

Nice to meet you Kara.

They shake hands.

KARA

You gave me some great input on saving time in our business that I did not gain in college that addresses our perticular business. I enjoyed your speech very much and will be using many of your ideas.

MR. PETER DASH

Glad to be of help and always nice to get such feedback from the seminars.

Mr. Peter Dash turns back to Linda.

MR. PETER DASH

Would you like to accompany me to dinner and we can talk about what you missed? I know a great place and I can answer any questions you may have.

LINDA

I don't think I should.

MR. PETER DASH

We all have to eat right? Why not join me.

LINDA

I'm sorry. I need to get to those brochures before they're all gone.

Linda turns around and goes to another table in the back. Looking back to watch him walk away.

KARA

You should've gone. It was just dinner and you could've picked his brain a little. I did write questions along the way you could have asked and that would have made it a business meeting.

LINDA

I know, I just paniced between my feelings and our job besides he's married. I don't want to give anyone the wrong impression that could make his wife cancel us out as a huge client. We're new and must look at the bigger picture we hope to gain.

KARA

You're probably right. As always.

Linda is checking out the pamphlets.

LINDA

Look at some of these deals. I can see as we grow buying in the bulk prices can save us alot of money and fresh always adds to the taste.

Kara shows the back of the pamflet to Linda as they continue to walk and have refreshments.

KARA

Look at this. It says if we order a hundred dollars or more they deliver for free within a ten mile radious. Saving us money and time. Can't beat that!

LINDA

We'll have to keep track of the price changes as they happen and what is in season as we go. Always working with what is in season will also help us save money. The more we can save the more we get to keep for things that always seem to come up or we need new.

KARA

Their website will do that for us. I'll set it up on the computer as one of our favorites when we go back into the office.

LINDA

Let's go check the market out tomorrow say about ten. We'll put the website up on the computor before we go. It'll give us prices for what is in season for our banquets we have coming up.

FADE OUT:

FADE IN:

EXT: Next day. mid-morning. Farmers market. Talking as they walk.

KARA

Linda, I can fix you up with an old friend of mine from college. I don't know him that well because back then we were so busy trying to work hard to get our degrees, but he seems like a nice guy. Maybe it will get your mind off Mr. Peter Dash. Especially if we end up getting his Enterprise as a client.

LINDA

I do need a distraction. Just not sure this is the best time for it especially if we get the enterprise as a client. Oh why not. It won't hurt to see someone new and start slowly. Okay!

Kara is picking vegtables needed for the next catering gig as she puts them in the cart that Linda is pushing as she marks their prices in a notebook.

(continue)

Well I have to admit as uncomfortable as it was for me going to that seminar it was helpful for us. The smell and the taste of our food will be great with these. I like this!

FADE OUT:

FADE IN:

INT: Catering Kitchen. Putting market food in the refrigerator. Early afternoon.

KARA

Linda I called Tim on the way over here and it's still the weekend. He's agreed to a date tonight at the Bella Rose at 8pm.

LINDA

What? That's too soon.

KARA

I was not going to give you time to change your mind. Now go home and get ready. I'll finish up here. Go on.

Kara using hand motion to push Linda own her way.

FADE OUT:

FADE IN:

INT: Evening. Dinning room where hostess takes Linda to the table where Tim is waiting.

Tim see's them coming and stands to greet Linda.

TIM

You must be the college friend Linda. I'm Tim Knox and how are you this evening?

As Tim pushes her chair in.

LINDA

It's nice to finally put a face to the man Kara speaks so highly of.

TIM

Well, that sounds good. Kara tells me you two have a catering business together and were roomates in college. Sounds like you two have been friends for a long time.

LINDA

Yes. We were actually working for a catering business to pay for our college loans and decided we liked it so why not have our own business. We have built it from the ground up and have started expanding to more clients recently.

TIM

Wow. Working together like that must make you guys really close?

Waitress arrives to take their order. Tim looks at Linda and says what would you like?

LINDA

Well I see you have duck and I've never had duck so I'll try that with the caesar salad, and raspberry ice tea.

TIM

I'll have the ha with fries with regular salad and french dressing and a coke.

Tim and Linda look at each other to continue the earlier conversation.

LINDA

So yes. We've spent many holidays with each others family during our college years.

TIM

I see your adventurous ordering the duck when you never had it before. Is Kara as adventurous as you too?

LINDA

When your in the catering business you need to try new things to see if it may fit your own menu as you continue to grow as a business. Right now were trying to land a whole enterprise as a client and if we do we will need to keep adding to our menu to keep it fresh and interesting. It would be nice to be able to change it up every six months or so.

TIM

I see comitting to your work comes first with you two. Does Kara have a big family?

LINDA

She has twin younger sisters and an older brother.

Dinner arrives.

LINDA
(continuing)

Her parents are very sweet. They always invite me to every special occassion. They make you feel at home even when you first meet them. Her grandma will always leave you in stitches when telling stories. She will keep you wondering whats true and whats not. She is so much fun and always makes the trip worth taking. Gives you something to talk about all the way home.

TIM

Sounds like a lady I need to meet.

LINDA

I get the feeling you really like Kara.

You see Tim shake his head up and down as he finishes chewing his salad.

TIM

To be honest, I've had my eye on Kara since college. We took accounting classes together. She would bump into me a lot because of how much she rushed around. It was quite cute. One time we had bumped so hard that we dropped our books together and while sorting them out we bumped our heads. I remember that one hurt. The our eyes met and I've been hooked on her since.

LINDA

So maybe you should've gone on a date with her instead?

TIM

After college I tried many times, but she seemed so focused on work all the time she would say she has her dream job so she won't give me the time of day for a date. I thought this would be a good way to try to maybe convince you to help me?

LINDA
(Laughing)

This is certainly a unique way to get her attention. Date the friend or do you have an angle here your hoping to play out?

TIM

Can you blame me. She's an amazing woman. I just want a chance for a good sit down conversation with her. The last year of college all I could do was watch her from a distance and after that see her in town at the coffee shop where again she was rushing.

Linda using her fork as motion when she talked.

LINDA

You know this would serve her right for trying to set me up and it's something her Grandma would do. We have a busy weekend coming up, but are you free next Wednesdy night?

TIM

Yes, Thanks I'll make the time. I just want her to stop the rushing around so she can notice me and take some time to relax so I can tell her how I have felt about her from that first bump.

LINDA

That is so sweet I have to take part in this. I'll tell her to meet me here at 8pm. So she can taste the food to see if we can add something new to our menu and organize our plan for the next banquet. You take it from there and tell her I felt you two should try a few things together and give a full report on what food flavors you both thought were best.

TIM

Thanks for this. I owe you and sorry again about this date. I'm glad you to are such good friends and thanks for being so understanding.

LINDA

That's fine anyhow this duck is a bit dry, but very tasty It was worth the meal assuming it's on your dime.

They both start laughing.

TIM

For sure! Were going to make good friends.

Tim walks Linda out and gives her a hug of gratitude.

LINDA

Now don't be late. Kara is always on time or ten minutes early.

FADE OUT:

FADE IN:

INT: Late morning. Banquet hall entrance board says guest speakers Susan Dash and Peter Dash with a picture of the two of them. Linda and Kara both stop and stares at it for a moment.

LINDA

See Kara, I told you he was married. Look how beautiful she is.

As Linda and Kara set up for lunch.

KARA

So how was your date last night?

LINDA

What a great guy. Tim is soft spoken, kind and had such a good sense of humor that he reminded me a bit of your Grandma. A very open guy not afraid to talk about his feelings and dreams for his future. Definetly know what he wants.

KARA

Really?

LINDA

Yeah he was so joyful and full of life. The food there was very unique too. I never had duck and I gave it a try. I was thinking of maybe taking one of their dishes and putting our own twist on it for one of our banquets.

(continue)

I made a reservation for tonight at 8pm. so we could go and try something we don't already have on the menu and figure out a dish or two to work with. If we get the enterprise gig were going to have to refresh our menu from time to time so people don't get the same food all the time. That can get old so we got to move up our game. You in?

KARA

That sounds great. Now let's get this luncheon up and ready.

As lunch is being served Linda gets curious and tries to get a live look at Susan Dash. Linda is in the corner of the banquet room as Kara walks up to her.

KARA

Linda, what are you doing?

They start walking back to the kitchen.

LINDA

His wife is so gorgeous.

KARA

Yes, she is and that style of clothes explains what you were saying very nicely. Don't worry we'll get there ourselves with hard work. Look at it as our future. Now lets get this place cleaned up so we can get to our tasting dinner night. I'm starved and haven't eaten yet today.

Linda and Kara start cleaning up in the kitchen. When Susan Dash walks in toward them.

SUSAN DASH

Ms. Hill that was delicious. Peter and I would like you to handle all of our fundraiser events and banquets. He's waiting for you outside to talk more about our vision on how we run our Enterprise. We'd also like to get know you a little better as you join our team.

Linda and Kara look at each other with a big smile but in control.

LINDA

Kara can you handle things here while I go speak to Mr. Dash? If you get done before I do don't forget our reservation at 8pm.

Kara is shaking her head at Linda.

KARA

Got it. See you at 8pm.

FADE OUT:

FADE IN:

EXT: Late afternoon. Linda goes out to find Mr. Peter Dash standing by a horse drawn carriage. Linda stops before walking out the door and looks confused. Talking out loud to herself

LINDA

His wife told me to so it must be okay!

Linda continues to walk out the door to the horse drawn wagon.

FADE OUT:

FADE IN:

INT: Susan Dash walks back into the kitchen to talk with Kara.

SUSAN

Hi, I forgot to give Linda her clothes. Peter had them dry cleaned for her. Could you be so kind as to give them to her.

Kara takes the clothes and as she is hanging it says.

KARA

That was so nice of your husband to do.

SUSAN

Oh no, Peter's not my husband he's my brother. We're jointly running the family business our parents started when they were our age.

Kara gets excited and with a smile says.

KARA

Please excuse me I've got to try to catch Linda before she goes with Mr. Dash she though he was your husband and has push him away so many times.

Susan seems just as excited as Kara and with a clap of her two hands together with a smile says.

SUSAN

By all means go!

With a hand gesture Susan is pushing her off to go. You see Kara running to the door to tell Linda and see that the horse drawn carriage is pulling away. As linda watches the carriage go Susan has caught up and is at the door with Kara.

KARA

I'm sorry I didn't mean to babble that out like that. That was not very proffessional of me to do so.

SUSAN

I'm so glad you did. Peter has been wondering why Linda has been pushing him away to not even go for coffee. It all makes sense now. It's sweet and loyal of her.

KARA

I hope somehow she finds out before a beautiful night ride in the city is ruined.

SUSAN

Me too. We've worked so hard to get to this point in our lives it's time we pay attention to ourselves and build a home life now that we have such a great business life.

KARA

I hear you there!

FADE OUT:

FADE IN:

INT: Evening. Bella Rose Dining room. Waitress takes Kara to the table Tim is seated at.

Kara slides into the seat before Tim even has a chance to stand up to push her chair in.

KARA

Oh, hi Tim. Linda didn't mention you'd be joining us.

TIM

Well, she won't actually be joining us, but she does expect a full report. She felt it would be nice for us to talk and wanted outside opinion on taste.

KARA

I didn't know that tasting food was one of your specialties. I seem to remember accounting was the world for you and you were so good at it.

TIM

Well let's order and we will see. She suggested we both order different items and we can sample off each others so we can discuss the flavors and how you might be able to change it to make it better to add to your menu. Linda had noticed they had sample dishes for those who like a variety. Let's get a couple of those. You can do the report.

Kara gives a little giggle.

KARA

Sounds good I'll do the seafood one.

TIM

I'll do the meat lovers and we probably should do a pasta one so we have everything covered for the report. What would you like to drink?

KARA

We better stick to water so we can better sample the food. The samples look small in the picture but enough to cut each in half so we can both try each for the report. Oh this is going to be fun. Thanks for taking part in this. I'm sure you have better things to do.

Kara lets Tim give the order.

KARA

Now why would Linda set this up and not be here to give her own input? She's more of the chef afterall. I am more of the book keeper in this business deal as you may have already guessed from our college days.

TIM

I agreed to a date with Linda so I could finally have a way to have a conversation with you. I've had my eyes on you since college. I just couldn't ever get you to slow down and take a break for yourself and notice me. So she helped me and here we are on the adventure of tasting good food.

KARA

So Linda knows all this and set this up?

TIM

Yes, she said you needed a break and that this is something your Grandma would've done for you. So let's enjoy this evening out. This is still technically you working and helping the business after all.

(Laughing)

KARA

Well she's right about one thing. This is right up grandma's alley and she'd laugh and talk about it for days and will when she finds out. I'm sure Linda will fill her in on every little detail for a good laugh. This one will brighten Grandma's day.

TIM

Linda did say she enjoys making people laugh. She sounds like a gem.

KARA

Here comes our dinner. We can take turns trying each others and seeing what we taste and like about each one.

TIM

Sounds like a good plan.

Tim let Kara start and decide which to taste first.

KARA

Lets start with the lobster we have in butter and in a sauce. So what do you do for a living Tim?

TIM

I'm an accountant at the JP accounting firm downtown.

KARA

I should have guessed that with you being at the top of the class. So what do you think of the lobster?

TIM

I liked the buttered one, but the sauced one has a very different flavor that may not appeal to a lot of people.

Kara is taking notes.

KARA

I agree. The buttered one you can taste a drop of vinegar that bring the lobster flavor out more as the sauce one hides the flavor of the actual lobster.

TIM

Boy your good at this and so detailed, but your right I did taste that tang in the buttered one. I thought it was the freshness of the lobster. Now lets try my broiled steak. Steak is always best right off the grill.

KARA

There you go. You'll know food enough to help me with our business all the time. Those little bits of details make a huge difference in my business.

TIM

I'd be glad to be part of the team for that. I'd never go hungry!

KARA

That would never happen in this business. So did you ever get a wife or have any kids.

TIM

No, I've had my eyes on you all along and tried so many times to talk to you when we meet on the street, but just couldn't get your attention. Boy this steak is really juice and tender. So easy to eat and not hard chewing at all. I like this one.

Kara is shaking her head in agreeance as she continues to take in the flavors. Putting a finger up as to say wait a minute.

KARA

Yes very juicy and you can tell it had been marinated with hickery BBQ sauce witha hint of terriaki sauce. I can taste both flavors in there. So how long have you been with the firm?

Kara is taking notes.

TIM

Fresh out of college and now thinking of buying my first home out by the lake for relax time on the water to unwind from work on the weekends.

KARA

Well seems like your doing well for yourself. Now we have haddock. Breaded and in a sauce.

Kara cuts it in half and when she pick it up to give him half it breaks leaving just a bit size on the fork and decides to feed it to him. Their eyes meet and they stay that way for a while.

TIM

If it breaks apart that easily we know it's fresh. I like looking into your eyes so I might need another piece to taste it right.

They both start to laugh.

KARA

I intended to give you the rest of the piece that broke off, but yes surely fresh.

Kara takes a bite.

(continue)

Very flakey. I like this. I think they used Panko for the crunch.

TIM

This is a toss up. I like the sauce one too. A little like a stew but not a stew. Do you want to go house hunting by the water with me this weekend?

KARA

Well I guess if I can feed you I can house hunt with you. Now lets try some of the pasta.

Tim gives a good laugh on that one.

TIM

Well then that's a date. I like a good baked mac and cheese lets try that one first.

They both take their forks and dig into the mac and cheese together. Looking up at each other with a smile.

KARA

The trick to a good mac and cheese is to firgure out what combination of cheese work best and it needs to be gouey. I can taste the cheddar cheese and American cheese in this one and the milk that helps make the sauce.

TIM

I think theres a little velveta cheese in there that give it that smoothness and maybe that panko on top for that crunch.

KARA

Very good. You best remember Linda is the cook not me. Now lets try a cold pasta. This one looks very well balance. Pasta, cucumber, tomatoes, chicken. Looks pretty simple lets see the flavor of the dressing.

TIM

Miracle whip. I know that taste anytime. This is more like a game then a job and a tasty one at that.

KARA

Right with a touch of ranch dressing to give it that zaz.

TIM

I don't know about you, but I'm full. How about we go to the other side of this room and end the night with a drink and maybe a dance.

KARA

Sounds perfect to me.

You watch them sip on a drink and get on the dance floor for a slow dance.

FADE OUT:

FADE IN:

EXT: Still evening going back to the horse drawn carriage with Linda and Mr. Peter Dash.

MR. PETER DASH

Linda I like your people skills and the softness about you. I've notice how you treat your employees as if you're all one big family. In a business that speaks a lot about you as a person.

LINDA

Thank you. The effort of my employees makes me a successful person. Showing and giving them respect has allowed me to keep my employees as long as I have. The input and advice are always appreciated and heard.

MR. PETER DASH

I not only wish for you to handle all of our banquets, but I would like to see if maybe things could work out for us as well.

Peter puts his hands on Linda's hands.

LINDA

Stop, Please.

Pulls her hands away and stands up almost falling on Peter when the horse stops.

MR. PETER DASH

What's wrong? I only meant that I find you to be a special person. Not someone you run into everyday. I would really like to get to know you more. Maybe even have a proper date.

LINDA

I'm just a little confused as to what makes you think I'm the type of person that would date a married man.

Peter puts both his hands out while still sitting himself.

MR. PETER DASH

Linda, I'm not married? Who told you I was married?

LINDA

I... I thought Susan Dash was your wife? You have a closet full of woman's clothes...

MR. PETER DASH

Susan....(Laughs) Susan is my sister.

LINDA

Oh.... wait... she's your sister? Oh I'm so sorry. I just assumed since she had the same last name and lived with you...

MR. PETER DASH

Will you just sit down now.

Peter pats the seat beside him.

Linda shyly sits down as they share a smile looking into each other's eyes.

(continues)

Charlies you may continue now.

LINDA

I guess everything makes more sense now. I'm really glad you're not married.

(Laughs)

MR. PETER DASH

Well, now your actions and being distant from me makes sense. I didn't realize I gave you that impression. Now tell me why your glad I'm not married ?

LINDA

To be honest I had a crush on you even before I knew your name. Then when I saw a picture of you and Susan I just assumed you were husband and wife and worked real hard to fight my feelings. My business partner even set me up on a date with a college friend of hers to distract me.

MR. PETER DASH

How did that work out?

LINDA

He agreed to a date with me to get a date with her. (Laughing) long story.

MR. PETER DASH

Oh, this has got to be good, do tell.

You see Linda relax and take his hand into hers.

LINDA

Well the short story is we were both working our way through college focussing on a career. Kara was very driven and she never seemed to give herself any form of social life. Always in a rush she did bump into people on occasion and when she bumped into Tim their eyes met and he's been in love with her ever sense. Tim has been in love with her for seven years. She has never given him the time of day every time they meet in town she was too busy to really have time with him. Poor guy was still trying. So when she called him for a date with me for my distraction from you he accepted.

MR. PETER DASH

So where does that leave you now?

LINDA

I returned the favor and set them up on a date. Any man who's in love for that long deserves to at least be notice and the rest is up to them. At least she has to sit with him and talk.

47

MR. PETER DASH

Is she going to be upset with you?

LINDA

I put them on a business tasting job together and wanting a full report. Kara being so determined for the business will go for it and I made it very clear to Tim he needs to tell her how he feels as he may not ever get another chance. Their on that date right now.

MR. PETER DASH

Now that was a smart smooth move. I'll have to keep an eye on you.

LINDA

Got to help a man who's loved a woman for that long and it's time for her to have a personal life now that we have our business rolling.

MR. PETER DASH

Speaking of love life can we have a real date now?

LINDA

Yes, I would like that.

They arrive back at the banquet hall. Peter gets off the carriage and puts his hand out to assist Linda down off the carriage.

MR. PETER DASH

Can I pick you up say around ten tomorrow and we can ride out to the country and have a picnic. Just enjoy the foliage and talk some more.

LINDA

Lovely I'll put on my walking shoes. See you in the morning. Good night.

MR. PETER DASH

Good night dear!

Peter watches Linda go into the building.

FADE OUT:

EXT: Tim arrived at the catering hall to pick up Kara.

TIM

Good morning Kara I trust you slept well last night.

Tim opens the car door to let Kara in then goes around to get in himself.

KARA

I feel like royalty riding in this classic mustang.

TIM

Fords do make good cars. This is a 1968 6 cylinder engine. I had to fix the distribution block that was leaking brake fluid when I first got it. Other then that mostly little things like adjusting the parking brakes. All in all this one was easy to get back on the road.

KARA

I like the color. Would they call it red or burgundy?

TIM

It's registered as burgundy. I wanted it to match the color with the age so theres a little mix in there, but I went with burgundy for registration purposes.

KARA

Classics are the best and yes I slept like a feather last night. I'm not use to drinking at all.

TIM

Oh sorry I'll keep that in mind. My first classic car was a covert and now I have six. They all have original parts with original paint colors redone. That is my hobby and I enjoy going to car shows to show them off. So you may see me pick you up in different cars.

KARA

I look forward to that. So now your into house hunting for your cars.

Tim starts to laugh.

TIM

In a way yes. The storage barn I've been using has a leak that's not good for the cars so I need my own place for them to protect them. I've sank a lot of money in them and want to preserve them.

KARA

Did you make a list of must haves when looking for your house.

TIM

The list is in my head. I pretty much know space wise how much room I need with work space. If the house is good but not the garage I need land enough to build a long bay garage for them which would be the best scenario for them.

KARA

Any other must haves before we start looking.

TIM

Don't want a fixer upper. I don't have time for that and no run down appliances. I would like three bedrooms and a porch over looking the water. If you were buying a house what would you want it to have or not have.

KARA

I of course would want appliances to be in good working order with a nook in the kitchen big enough for baking pies. A private bathroom in the master bedroom. The rest I can turn into a home from there.

TIM

A women with only a few natural wants. I like that and the pie too. Here we are at the first one.

They start with taking a walk around the outside of the house.

TIM

I don't see any point in checking the inside of this one. The roof is very bad so the house must have water damage. The siding was a poor job you can clearly see on the back here. Let's move on.

You watch them go back into the car and driving away.

KARA

That house did not have much life left in it. As we went around the corner I notice the back wall did not look straight. I think the roof problem went there.

TIM

Kara, hun if you notice things like that please feel free to say something. This is a big investment and I truly want your input on this. Just say it the way you see it. Don't go shy on me now. I value your input. Here is the next one.

They get out of the car and do a walk around.

KARA

Roof looks new and walls are straight. Oh a cute little porch to sit on to watch the sunset and listen to the water.

TIM

Looks good, but I don't see a garage. Let's find out how much land this comes with and check the inside out. If there's enough land I can build my bay garage for the cars on the side of the house and not interfere with your porch view at all.

KARA

I hope it has my kitchen.

Kara was excited to see the kitchen and was checking the appliances out when Tim comes in the kitchen.

TIM

I heard that word my kitchen. I like the sound of that. So what do you think? Is this the style kitchen you're looking for?

KARA

Yes and all the appliances are in working order just not the modern style I would prefer, but that can be easily changed. Where did you go?

TIM

I was talking to the relestate agent and told her what we both were looking for and she told me her co-worker has an open house just a few houses down the road that might be just what we want. She also gave me this pamphlet of other houses along this lake side we might want to check out. This one doesn't have the land for me to build my garage bays for the cars.

KARA

Well then Let's go!

You watch Kara and Tim drive two houses down the road.

TIM

This looks better already. Let's check it out.

They both eagerly jump out of the car not waiting for door opening from Tim.

KARA

A bigger house for sure, but bigger means more money.

Kara stops a minute to see Tim's face wondering if that's a problem.

TIM

Yes, come on. That's not a problem for me. It just went on the market. It's owned by an old couple who are down sizing. The great part is she was a school teacher teaching homeech and he was a mechanic.

As they walk into the house Kara's eyes open wide. She grabs Tim's arm and says.

KARA

Look at this kitchen and all the cupboards. She must have really enjoyed cooking for sure. The appliances are up to date.

TIM

That was done for the sale from what this flier says as it was converted from gas. Kara we forgot to do the walk around outside first.

KARA

I'm sorry I ran ahead of you.

TIM

I wouldn't want it any other way, but my main goal is to have a place for my cars. Let's check the master bedroom and see if it has a private bathroom to finish your want list then lets check outside. Okay!

KARA

Sure babe let's do that.

Kara mellowed out some.

TIM

You have your private bath and it's a neutral color. From what the brochure says there is a half bath on this main floor too and two bedrooms upstairs with another full bath.

KARA

That sounds perfect. Did you notice the hard wood floors and the fireplace in the living room on the way to the master bedroom?

TIM

I did see a cozy night by the fire place with a piece of pie.

Kara grabs Tim by the arm and says.

KARA

Let's go see if they have your list of wants outside.

You see Kara and Tim do a walk around.

TIM

So far I like the wide driveway and away from the road some. The garage is not big enough for my cars. Let's check the back to see how much land there is out back for me to build one. I'm assuming these trees are property lines.

They walk to the back and you see a disappointing look on Tim's face.

KARA

The roof is good and the walls are straight. Look at the porch. Much wider then the last one for BBQ'n and just relaxing as we watch the sunset go down after a day of work. Whats wrong Tim?

TIM

There is no room for the bay garage I need for my cars here. Will have to keep looking babe. Sorry!

Tim grabs Kara and gives her a side hug in a way to comfort her from the disappointment.

KARA

No problem your cars come first on this adventure. That was your main reason for house hunting. What do we have next in that brochure.

TIM

Oh I think the clouds have another plan for us. Here comes the rain.

They run to the car and get in.

(continues)

Will you come back with me next Sunday and look at more houses? I'm looking for the perfect one for a lifetime. I'm not much of a move around person and wish to have all my wants the first time around. I hope we can find one with land to do things on. Don't want to be crowded up close to others.

They start driving back to the catering hall.

KARA

Of course I will. This was fun and I can't wait to see what you end up choosing. I enjoyed myself today. It was a refreshing break for me that I haven't had in a long time just like last night.

TIM

What we end up choosing. I want you to be as much a part of finding the right fit as a fit for me and the cars. It may be a new relationship to you, but I've been in love with you and watching you for seven years. I truly feel like we are a good match.

KARA

I like how we are together too.

TIM

Want to grab a bite to eat before heading back I know a great pub that serves great sandwiches. There's BBQ rib sandwiches that are great and so is the chicken one.

KARA

Okay just a sandwich I have a lot of paperwork to get done tonight to start the week with out big new enterprise client.

TIM

Well there we have something to celebrate.

They park and walk into Pete's pub.

KARA

Hey will you look at that. You say this is your favorite pub?

TIM

Yes. It's my favorite Saturday night hang out place to get great food and relax at the end of the week. Why?

Kara and Tim place their order.

KARA

See that picture on the wall. That's Mr. Peter Dash our new client and this is his pub.

TIM

What a small world. Now wait a minute is that the guy Linda went on a date with.

KARA

Yes it is and I wonder how that went. Can't wait for work tomorrow to get the scoop.

TIM

Our order is up I'll go get it.

Tim returns and they begin to eat.

(continues)

Well good for her. So tell me Kara what is the scoop on us going to sound like tomorrow.

KARA

Nothing, but some good old honest truth.

FADE OUT:

FADE IN:

Ext: Peter is driving his own car when he picks up Linda for there ride in the country. Linda carries a fall jacket with her and her camera incase.

MR. PETER DASH

Good morning Linda. I've chosen a perfect spot by the lake viewing a gorgious mountain with beautiful foilage for our picnic.

Peter opens the car door for Linda to get in and off they go.

LINDA

We surely have a nice sunny day for it that will brighten the view. The perfect time doesn't last long when we have rain coming for the next few days. I do enjoy fall very much. It feels peaceful in some way.

MR. PETER DASH

Your right on that one. Now we have to make one quick stop at my favorite pub to pick up our picnic basket on the way. I hope red wine is fine with you?

LINDA

I'm not much of a drinker, but I'm sure that will be fine.

They get to the pub and Peter goes in to get the picnic basket as Linda sits in the car and checks the place out. Linda takes notice to the name of the pub

Peter comes out and puts the basket in back and on their way they go again.

MR. PETER DASH

All set, now tell me how did your partners night go last night?

LINDA

I haven't heard a thing so everything must have worked out find. I'm sure Kara would have called if it hadn't. I did expect a call this morning, but

(continue)

still hadn't. I did tell Tim if she questioned my thoughts, to tell her I did what her grandma would have done in my place. That would surely give her a laugh and break the ice.

Mr. PETER DASH

You two are really good friends and I'm not sure what all that grandma stuff means, but I'm sure in time I will. Here we are.

LINDA

WOW ! What a view I've got to get a few pics of this.

While Linda is taking pictures Peter is laying down a blanket and setting up the picnic.

(continue)

I'm sorry I should have helped you out first. I like taking my own pictures and getting them developed to hang for sale in my banquet hall. Just a little side hobby and want the memories of beauty. I do sell quite a few of them.

MR. PETER DASH

Always thinking. Something we have in common.

Peter has taken the liberty of laying out cheese and fresh fruits with a glass of red wine and while Linda is putting her camera away and sitting down on the blanket Peter hands her a glass of red wine.

LINDA

Thank you!

Linda takes a sip of wine as they face the mountain.

(continue)

What does the Peter Dash Enterprise consist of? What is your business all about?

MR. PETER DASH

Like yourself I'm in the food industry, but have grown to a much wider scale then just serving like our parents did. Susan and I are very good speakers so a few years back we decided to grow our business by helping others as well as ourselves.

LINDA

The loaded question would be how if you don't mind my asking. I know Susan has us packing all leftovers for the food shelter as a way to give back is that what your taking about?

Linda and peter are staring still at the foliage and sipping their wine as they continue to talk.

MR. PETER DASH

Oh it's so much more then that my dear. That's Susan's little extra. We have a number of Pubs around this state and surrounding states.

LINDA

Like Pete's Pub that we stopped at to pick up our basket.

MR. PETER DASH

You pay attention to details. I like that and yes. That is one of mine. Susan and I take turns naming them as we acquire them. That is how we continue to grow the business are parents started. So you see we know good tasting food when we have it. So your Cordon Blue made it high on our list. Not only that, but you was serving to restaurant owners as well.

LINDA

Oh my goodness! Now you really making me nervous. I'm so glad I didn't know that before, I would have been a wreck.

MR. PETER DASH

Don't be! Now you know you got what it takes to make it. Many other know it too. If you have confidence in yourself and what you're doing it shouldn't bother you at all. You should see the look on your face right now. That would be a picture to frame up.

A moment of silence and a few sips more of wine for Linda.

LINDA

You're right I do and you just gave me more to bank on. Thanks for that!

MR. PETER DASH

Your welcome. For us Susan is big on nutrition and that's her part in our seminars and what we found is a lack in fresh produce in the communities that our Pubs are in so we took it upon ourselves to do something about it.

LINDA

That's where the farmers market come in. Right? I've got to say, we went last Saturday and found a big savings for us and that will get even bigger now that we have your enterprise. I found the meat department was low though. We're big on chicken.

MR. PETER DASH

Well my dear if you would have come with me for coffee I could have explained how that goes. I'm sure your partner must have it in her notes. Only low amounts get put in the market to give you a sample of what the farmer has, but you can order what you want or go to their shops to pick

(continue)

what you want. It's about keeping meats fresh at the right temperature and safe for consumption.

LINDA

I'll have to ask Kara about that. I did not find pamphlets on that at your seminar at the college.

MR. PETER DASH

That was part one covering fruits and vegetables. Their attention is only so long before it becomes boring for them. The nutrition part and most important part is pretty long.

LINDA

I can see that with the proper caring and storing at right temperature for longer lasting food.

MR. PETER DASH

Yes, but there's a lot more to it then just that. We needed more farmers and for them to grow what we needed to keep our Pubs supplied with fresh produce all year long.

LINDA

Have you accomplished the goal of all year long? How long have you been doing this?

MR. PETER DASH

Ten years if that's your way of trying to find out how old I am.

They both break out laughing as Peter refills their glass.

LINDA

I wasn't thinking that, but I am now. Got it!

MR. PETER DASH

We teamed up with local colleges in the agricultural department and learned how to write up grants for our plans using students for hands on learning with the hope of gaining future farmers to meet our fresh produce needs. Not only for us, but others in the food industry line of work. We all need to help save the farms and get young people into farming for the future.

LINDA

That is so amazing. I regret being late for that seminar now.

MR. PETER DASH

As you should. Now try some of this shrimp Alfredo with broccoli. We have a chocolate cake for dessert.

LINDA

Oh this is good. I like that they used small shrimp so you almost get one on every bite and the sauce is light but not drippy. Nice! So do you teach at the college too?

MR. PETER DASH

No I'm more like a connector.

LINDA

Connector? What on earth is that suppose to mean?

MR. PETER DASH

I connect the agricultural students with Farmers in the community. I find farmers who are willing to produce what we lack at the farmers markets. The grants we collect help to pay for soil testing so it meets the needs of what we want to grow and supply it to the farmers. We also collect farm work grants so in the summer these students can work the land as farmers do to grow the produce. It's a win for the learning of the students with a paid summer job and farmers are happy to have the help.

LINDA

So it's a win for the farmers and the community not to mention those of us in the food industry. I admire what your doing. Give the students a good idea of what farming is all about and if that is the life they want to pursue after college. Kind of like Kara and I who worked for a catering business paying our way through college and decided to do it for ourselves after college. Now let's get some of that cake.

Peter reaches into the basket for the individual packed cakes and forks and gives one to Linda.

MR. PETER DASH

Retaining those farmers we have and get these agricultural students interested in it for the future one community at a time is our big goal on top of getting everyone working together like a well oiled machine.

LINDA

You know looking back at my days in high school most students did learn better with hands on and when schools cut those programs out we saw a lot of drop outs. So I appreciate very much what your doing. This cake is great by the way.

MR. PETER DASH

My Pubs make everything on site fresh themselves and this pub is very good at making cakes. Everything a day old Susan sends to the food shelter. She does her part to better the community in different ways than I, but we love sharing for having been blessed so much.

Linda and Peter continue to eat the cake while looking at the foliage.

(continue)

I must say I'm proud of what were doing in the community. It's been hard especially at first to connect it all up, but in the long run has made our seminars very popular.

LINDA

So exactly how do you connect it all to your seminars?

MR. PETER DASH

I have a website for all caterers, restaurants, hotels and even airlines to connect with us along with people in the community. They let us know what their produce needs are what they have trouble finding and need for their recipes. When I work with farmers I try to meet those needs and I hold seminars to inform the people about the quality in a nutritional way and cost of the new produce.

(continue)

Those paying to attend the seminar get a one time ten percent discount card on the new items from the farmers. There way of introducing themselves and drumming up continued business. Farmers are always willing to pay it forward for all the future sales to come. Vendors are happy to come to the seminars and they get more than just their money back with the one time discount card they get for attending not to mention your fine cooking.

LINDA

Thank you for that. It all seems to go full circle doesn't it.

MR. PETER DASH

That's business! It all works and everyone is happy and the way I see it, it's a well working together community.

LINDA

Well I never took agriculture in college, but I sure have learned a lot today. Are you sure you're not some kind of professor?

MR. PETER DASH

No! No! That's not for me I'm more of a people person and enjoy talking to the farmers. I've saved a lot of farms from going under and we need them all. That's been my joy in life until I met you.

LINDA

Oh my, look up at the clouds. We better pack this up we're about to get rained on.

They start packing fast and run to the car just as the rain comes pouring down heavy. Half out of breath they get in the car catching their breath and laughing.

(continue)

We made it!

Sitting in the car Peter looks at Linda and says.

MR. PETER DASH

I enjoyed today and our talk even though I may have talked your ear off. It was very relaxing which is new to me and the foliage was at it's peak.

LINDA

I agree the relax time was well over do and I got some lasting pictures of the foliage that I can't wait to frame up. The conversation was enlightening and leaves me admiring you even more.

Peter sits facing Linda and takes her hand saying.

MR. PETER DASH

Well thank you for today. I hope we can do this again only more about you next time. I do need to work on fair balance conversation. So for that I apologize, sometimes I just talk to much part of being a speaker I guess.

A little giggle there.

LINDA

You were just fine. You had my interest and I'm blown away with all you have accomplished in ten years. It would take most people a lifetime to get all that put together, but you're a very driven man. I like that a lot and I'd be honored to do this again.

Peter straightens himself up and starts the car and drives back.

LINDA

I hope things worked out great last night for Kara and Tim. I just checked my phone and still nothing from her. I hope they decided to do something together today and I'll hear about it at work tomorrow.

MR. PETER DASH

I don't know him, but I hope after all those years of loving her that they did hit it off and made a day of it like we did.

LINDA

That we did!

MR. PETER DASH

Now lets see If we can find a parking space. I'm not use to parking my own car in town.

Linda gives a little laugh.

LINDA

You'll get use to it. Oh look there's one behind the red car.

Linda is pointing to the spot. They park and Peter goes around to open Linda's door. As Linda steps out she see's Kara and Tim coming from the other end of the street. They are walking towards each other and stop in front of the catering business.

(continue)

I see things must have worked out for you Tim.

TIM

Yes, and for that I couldn't thank you enough.

Linda goes to introduce Tim to Peter.

LINDA

Peter this is Tim. Tim this is Peter from Peter Dash Enterprise.

The two men shake hands.

MR. PETER DASH

I heard a lot about you Tim and glad to see you finally got a sit down with the love of your life.

TIM

I take it you know how a set up date got twisted around grandma style.

Everyone has a little laugh.

MR. PETER DASH

Yes, in a very romantic way I may ad.

TIM

We just ate at Pete's pub. I didn't know that was your place. I've been a regular there on Saturday night for years.

MR. PETER DASH

A return customer is always nice to hear. Thanks!

KARA

From what I see here you found out he wasn't married to Susan after all. Peter you'll be glad to hear Susan was also happy for you two.

Kara puts a thumb up pointing to Linda.

(continue)

Boy the day dreaming this girl was going through was hard to see all the time. I'm so happy things turned out right for you two.

MR. PETER DASH

Oh really!

As Peter turns and looks into Linda's eyes.

(continue)

We just came from a lovely picnic while looking at peak foliage before the rain that was only supposed to come tomorrow made an early arrival on us.

TIM

Kara and I just came from house hunting by the lake when it hit us.

Linda gets a puzzled look on her face.

LINDA

What?

TIM

Accounting for me has been going great and I have enough money tucked away and was already looking at places by the lake so I asked Kara to join me until the rain came, but we got some good viewing today and agreed to shop some more another day.

LINDA

Looks like we were both by the lake today. I'm surprised we didn't meet up there, but we were in one spot only. Did you take time to look at the foliage?

TIM

Yes we did as we sat on the porch checking out the view from one of the porches that made our list to consider buying.

LINDA

I got some good pictures for the wall to show you later. Oh my Kara look at the rainbow.

As the girls are looking up to the sky at the rainbow a car comes by and both men stand quickly in front of the girls to take the splash of the muddy water on their backside. You see the two girl notice what just happened and look at each other saying at the same time...

KARA and LINDA

Their Keepers

Kara and Linda then both give their man a kiss and that is how the movie ends with them kissing.

THE END

Main Characters:
Mr. Peter Dash - from Peter Dash Enterprise
Ms. Linda Hill - half owner of catering business
Ms. Kara Benson - other half owner of the catering business

Supporting Characters:
Susan Dash - Peter Dash's sister
Jennifer Hoss - Director of the Peter Dash Enterprise
Tim Knox - College friend
Small Parts:
Charles - Limo Driver
Doris - Maid
Hostess at the Bella Rose
3 Servers in the catering business

Scenes:

EXT: Outside by road of Catering Business

    By Limo Car
    Farmers Market
    Horse Drawn Carriage
    Picnic By The Lake

INT: Banquet Hall and Kitchen

    Catering Hall, Kitchen, and Office
    College Auditorium
    Bella Rose Dinning Room
    Mansion with Walk-In Closet
    Peter Dash's Head Office
    In Limo
    In Peter's Personal Car
    Tim's classic mustang

Viewing of three houses.

THE

END

Printed in the United States
by Baker & Taylor Publisher Services